Lucy's Umbrella

by sara madden

illustrated by hayley helsten

AuthorHouse™
1663 Liberty Drive
Bloomington, IN 47403
www.authorhouse.com
Phone: 1 (800) 839-8640

Published by AuthorHouse 04/11/2017

ISBN: 978-1-5246-8697-0 (SC)
ISBN: 978-1-5246-8698-7 (e)

Library of Congress Control Number: 2017905460

Print information available on the last page.

This book is printed on acid-free paper.

authorHOUSE®

"Never lose an opportunity for seeing anything that is beautiful."

— Ralph Waldo Emerson

This is Lucy. Lucy loves to wear different patterns, colors, and fabrics. She also likes to admire her reflection and the patterns on her skin. Each beautiful spot makes her who she is. Because Lucy lives in Seattle, she uses her umbrella nearly every day. Whenever Lucy finds something beautiful, she makes a note of it inside her umbrella to remind her of the beauty all around her.

Today, Lucy is going to the park to meet her mother for lunch. As she walks, the wind sweeps her umbrella away. She chases it to her friend, Lacey's, front yard. Lacey wears different colors on her clothes and in her hair. She likes to accessorize with as many different shades as possible. Lucy loves this about Lacey.

Lacey smiles, closes the umbrella, and hands it back to Lucy. "Thanks," Lucy says and hugs her. As she continues her way to the park, she takes out her pen and adds "Lacey's sense of style" to her umbrella of beautiful things.

On the path, Lucy notices some ladybugs on a small bush. She stops to admire the patterns on the little insects. She takes a moment to draw a ladybug on her umbrella and to write "so beautiful" under her drawing.

ME.

When it starts raining, Lucy opens her umbrella
and finds a frog inside. It hops onto the ground,
and Lucy admires the swirling shapes
on its skin. She laughs when it croaks.

She draws the frog on her umbrella and writes, "Brilliant."

butterflies

esses

earrings

Lucy's friend, Lorna, sees her on the path and runs to her side. They hold hands and jump over puddles together. Lorna has a talent for face painting. Today, she decorated her face with beautiful colors to look like a blue butterfly.

When Lorna leaves to go back home, she and Lucy wave goodbye. Lucy adds "Lorna's flare for imagination" to her umbrella.

Farther down the path, a tree lizard jumps onto Lucy's umbrella. She holds it carefully in her hands and looks at the stripes on its tail. After gently placing it on a nearby tree, Lucy draws a lizard on her umbrella.

At the park entrance, Lucy watches a bee land on a lilac bush. Both the bush and bee have colors and patterns that she adores.

When the bee flies away, Lucy smells the sweet flower.
Then, she draws a bee on her umbrella.

Once the rain stops, Lucy closes her umbrella, and a butterfly lands on her nose. She notices that its pattern is similar to the one on her hand.

She admires her hand and the butterfly. She writes "I am beautiful" on her umbrella.

Lucy sees her mom, Linda, waiting under the gazebo with their Dalmatian, Lizzy. Lunch is ready! She loves to see the park, in all its beauty, during this rainy spring day. She appreciates the new buds on the trees, the freshly grown grass, and the blossoming flowers.

Lucy and her mom share their sandwich,
Lucy getting the larger half. She hugs Lizzy,
who licks her face.

On their way home, Linda and Lucy hold hands under their umbrella. A rainbow appears over the horizon, and Lucy decides she will write about it on her umbrella when she gets home.

Later, Lucy invites Lacey and Lorna over.
They share pink marble cookies that Lucy's mom
made for them. They spend the rest of the afternoon
playing hopscotch, jump rope, and painting
each other's nails.

Our World

Our world is full of color. Our world is full of beauty.
But our world is not so full of peace, love, and unity.
I want our world to be a place where I can be free
To be unapologetically me.

At bedtime, her mom asks, "What did you find today, Lucy?" Lucy opens her umbrella and tells her mom about all of the wonderful things she found, all written on her special umbrella.

Hi there! It's Lucy! You may have wondered where I got the beautiful, unique spots on my skin. Well, let me tell you! I have a condition called vitiligo. Have you heard of it? If not, here are a few fun facts about it.

My dad, Tyler, helped me research this information online. He reminds me every day how lucky I am to be me.

1. Vitiligo happens when the cells that make the color on my skin are destroyed in certain areas. It's sort of like the opposite of freckles, where there are too many color cells in your skin. All it means is that in some places, I don't have my natural coloring on my skin.

2. Vitiligo is not contagious. Like freckles, some people have it, some people don't. Just ask my friends, Lacey and Lorna. We hold hands and give hugs all the time, but they don't have my special spots.

3. Vitiligo only affects the skin, and it is not dangerous. There is nothing wrong inside or outside of me. I just have a little more variety than most people on my skin.

If you would like to learn more about vitiligo, here are some great websites that will answer your questions:

https://www.avrf.org
https://www.niams.nih.gov/Health_Info/Vitiligo
http://vrfoundation.org

I love my vitiligo and the fun patterns that it has given my skin. Whether you have vitiligo, freckles, neither, or any other qualities that make you look different, just remember that you are special and beautiful exactly the way that you are!

- Lucy
xox♥

About The Author:

Sara Madden, who may or may not be a witch, grew up on California's Central Coast. She was raised on donuts and cookies provided by her grandparents' Tan Top Bakery. Her first story was written at age six, titled "I Love My Family," and she's been writing ever since.

Growing up dyslexic (and her continued fun with it into adulthood), Sara always has and always will find comfort in words, imagination, and believing in the unbelievable.

She currently lives in Utah with her adorable family, who may or not be completely bonkers. She has four unreliable guard dogs, eight clocks that refuse to tell time, and one unremarkable trampoline. Buttery popcorn and cinnamon cake donuts are her favorite food. And she never, ever, never, ever, never leaves home without a stick of vanilla or cake batter lip balm in her pocket (her tastes are undeniably fantastic!). In her spare time, she loves to paint and roller skate, but never at the same time-messes are dangerously unavoidable (she knows-she's tried it!).

Look for more of Sara Madden's books coming soon.

Follow Sara Madden and Tallulah Froom online at:
- SaraMaddenBooks.com
- TallulahFroom.com

About The Illustrator:

Hayley grew up painfully shy but full of wonder. Her cheesy but adorable parents and seven crazy siblings brought her love and laughter, but she rarely spoke outside her home until she was a teenager. She did, however, find plenty of opportunities to express herself, dancing everywhere she went and drawing on every surface she could find. She fought every day to be happier, healthier, and weirder.

Hayley has grown (slightly) taller and wiser since those days, but she still believes life's greatest joys are dancing in public, laughing until you cry, and eating chocolate chip cookies for dinner.

She now gets to enjoy life with her cute husband Jeffrey and their happy baby Lucy. They live part time in their small but cute home in Utah, and part time in their VW bus named Magnolia. Both homes are full of kisses and covered in illustrations of all kinds.

Check out more of Hayley's work at HayleyHelsten.com!